hurricanes & halloween

katrina marie

prologue

TODAY IS the last day I can respond. Yes or no…

There aren't any other surfaces for me to clean. The freezer is stocked and there isn't really a reason for me to be here. It's only an excuse so I don't have to answer my friends back home. They haven't stopped texting, and calling, since the invites were sent out.

"Why are you staring at your phone like it's a bomb about to blow up in your face?" Eric asks from the kitchen door.

I didn't even hear it open. Or, he's just that sneaky. He really needs a bell around his neck so we know when he's coming.

"I have to RSVP for my high school reunion." It's the one thing that's been plaguing my mind for months. I haven't been home in years, and the only thing keeping me away is my own fear. Fear of seeing her again. It's my own fault, but that's beside the point.

"That doesn't seem like a difficult decision." He is right behind me now. "You either want to, or you don't."

"Why are you even here?" He never comes back here

unless he wants me to make him something to go, or watch me over my shoulder.

It's only now that I've noticed the bar is quiet. "We're done with the cleanup, and ready to lock everything down. I didn't see you leave, and assumed you were still in here."

"Sorry, I'm ready to go." I glance toward the freezer I was looking in a few moments ago. "Just making sure I have everything I need for the next couple of days."

"Is this reunion the reason you've been staying late? And helping clean up?"

Always trying to get to the bottom of things, this one. There's no use avoiding the question, he'll keep pestering. "Yeah."

"If it's causing you this much stress, I say don't go. But you could always flip a coin and leave it to fate." He turns toward the door and walks out. Guess I'm locking up tonight. He does have a point though.

Digging around in my pocket, I listen for everyone to leave. The bar is quiet and I take a deep breath. At least nobody will be around to see me do this. Finally, a coin slips through the keys in my pocket, and I pull it out. This small piece of silver will decide if I go to the reunion, or not. Placing it on my thumb, I flick it into the air.

1

patrick

HOME LOOKS a lot different than it did when I was eighteen years old. The houses seem smaller, and more worn down. Maybe it's just because I've been gone for ten years.

Mom and Dad are sitting on the porch when I pull into the drive. Mom jumps out of her chair and rushes down the stairs. I barely have the truck door open before her arms are around me. "You made it."

Pushing the door back with my foot, I hug her. "I did. How long have y'all been waiting out here for me?"

"Oh, not long at all."

Dad moves beside her and waits until she lets me go. "Don't let her lie to you. It's been about an hour, and that's only because I made her wait that long."

"I bet."

Mom moves aside, and my dad wraps me in a tight hug. He must have really missed me because when I left all those years ago, all I got was a handshake. Even when they visit me in Asheville, he never puts this much emotion into our greetings or farewells.

"It's good to have you home, Son." Dad's voice is gruff as he pulls away. I guess I never realized just how much they missed having me around, despite coming to visit me in Texas.

"Thanks." I glance around the yard. The grass is a little tall, and there are things that need to be put away. A quick glance at my watch. I should have time to handle that before I head to the reunion. "It's okay that I stay here, right?"

"Don't be silly," Mom waves me away, "I'd be offended if you stayed in a hotel. Besides, the closest good ones are almost an hour away."

"You're right."

I grab my bag from the truck bed and follow them inside. Mom's cooking hits me as soon as I open the door. The herbs waft through the air, and her cooking is what made me want to be a chef.

"I hope you're hungry. It'll be ready in about an hour," she glances at the clock, "will you have time to eat before you meet your friends at the reunion?"

"There's always time for your cooking," I stop to kiss her on top of the head, "I'm going to put this in my room and go clean up the yard a bit for y'all."

"You don-" I don't give her time to finish the argument.

"I know. I want to." I added some buffer time to do just this for them. It's the least I can do for them while I'm here. Asking for someone who does yardwork is also on my list to talk to my friends about.

"Don't work yourself too hard."

"I won't."

I walk down the short hallway and toss my bag into my

room. I'll see what they've changed in my room when I come back inside, right now I want to get this done. It's the only thing that will keep my mind from wandering to Jaylen.

* * *

Alternative rock is blasting through the speakers as I enter the local bar. It's not as big as Out of the Ashes, but it's enough to hold my graduating class. At least that's what it feels like. Maybe there's just too much clutter everywhere.

"Patrick!" I look in the direction of my name being called. Hudson and Liam are, of course, leaning against the bar. I don't know why I expected to find them anywhere else.

There's an empty space between the both of them. I can only assume it's for me. The only problem is, there's a table by the door with a woman I vaguely remember standing behind it.

"Hey, Patrick," she waves me over, "glad to have you back for the reunion. Just grab one of those stickers and write your name on it."

For the life of me I can't remember her name. "Hey." Working in the bar, this is the best way I've found to greet people when I don't know names. "Thanks."

Quickly, I use the marker to write my name on the sticker, peel the back off and slap it on my chest. I know I've done the right thing when the woman nods and gives an appreciative smile. "Have a great night."

Vacating the area, I hurry toward my friends. Other people I went to school with wave at me, and I wave back. This is why I didn't want to come. Attention focused on me is unsettling. Especially since I went to culinary school instead of doing what the entire town hoped I would, and continue playing football.

"Long time no see," Hudson slaps me on the back, "I wondered if you were actually going to come."

"I definitely had my doubts." Even after I responded, I thought of a million different ways I could bail. I even tried to give Angie a lame excuse about being needed there. But she wasn't having it.

Liam bumps my shoulder, "I'm glad you came. It's been a while since we've hung out."

"Y'all are free to come to Asheville whenever you want. I have plenty of room."

"You realize that drive is long, and boring, right?" Hudson shakes his head.

"Flights aren't that expensive, and you're close enough to a major airport."

"Still," he waves his hands no, "I'd rather not."

"You never know what you might be missing, if you'd travel a bit. What's the point of staying in the same town you grew up in when there's a huge world out there for the taking."

I say all that as I ended up settling in a small town. It's different, though. Now that Out of the Ashes is *the* place to be in the area, we meet all sorts of people.

"I like it here," Hudson shrugs, "I'm a short distance from the city without all the people."

It makes sense. Changing his mind isn't going to happen anytime soon, if ever. Back in high school, he made it perfectly clear he was happy staying here to take over the family business.

"Besides," Liam laughs, "if you were here more often, you'd be able to catch up with Jaylen."

Why did he have to bring her up? She's the whole

reason I debated coming. We were best friends as kids. She was part of our friend group throughout high school. At least until I ruined things right before leaving for culinary school. If I had kept my mouth shut things wouldn't be weird between us.

"Jaylen's doing her own thing, and I'm doing mine. Me being here wouldn't change that."

"Are you sure about that?" Hudson grins.

"Yeah, why?"

"Because she just walked in with her friends, and she's heading straight for us." Liam laughs. He's supposed to be the one with reason, not the one about to put me in uncomfortable situations.

Turning toward the entrance, I see her. A big part of me wants to approach her and catch up. The other part wants to melt into the bar.

The choice is taken out of my hands completely because Liam is right. She's walking straight to us.

2

jaylen

"WHY ARE we here so early? You know the party doesn't get started until much later." Hannah asks as I park my car. We frequent this bar more often than I'd like to admit. It's the only place in town to hang out on the weekends when we don't feel like driving into New Orleans. Seems fitting to have our high school reunion here.

"You know why." I glance over at her. Patrick is really the only reason I wanted to come to this thing. Aside from the folks who moved off to do big wonderful things, I see most of the people on a daily basis. Kind of hard not to when you're teaching their kids.

"What if he isn't even here?" Kelly leans between us from the backseat. "Last I heard he hadn't given a response yet."

I guess it's a good thing I checked yesterday. "Amanda told me he did."

"Of course, she did." Kelly rolls her eyes before speaking again. "He may not even recognize you. Besides, didn't y'all leave things on uneven footing the last time you saw each other?"

Did she have to bring that up. It's not like it was completely his fault. I didn't know how to respond. He was my best friend. I didn't expect him to come out and say he had feelings for me. Though, I don't think he did either. It just sort of...happened.

"That doesn't matter," I groan and open the door, "we're adults now. Both of us are capable of having a rational conversation."

"If you say so." Hannah gets out of the car and Kelly follows. "Let's do this thing."

I will never understand why they are so hyped up about hanging out with people we see every day. But I'll let them have their fun since they haven't given me too much crap about Patrick.

Inhale. Exhale. I close my car door and turn toward my friends. "Let's go."

Our heels click against the pavement as we make our way across the parking lot to the bar. It's the beginning of what I hope to be a weekend of getting reacquainted with my former best friend.

Kelly pulls the door open, and the dim lighting is a stark contrast to the sun behind us. We file inside, and stop at the registration table. The three of us write our name in black sharpie on stickers before placing it on our chests. It does nothing for our outfits, but I understand why they do it.

Before I have a chance to ask Amanda if he's here. She nods and points in the direction of the bar. I peek my head around my friends and see him leaning against it with his friends.

"Thanks." I mouth to her. Moving around my friends, I straighten my back and take a step forward.

"How do you know this is going to work?" Hannah asks close to my ear to be heard over the music.

"I don't," I shrug off her question, "all I can do is hope."

Another glance at the bar, and Patrick is looking everywhere but in my direction. He definitely knows I'm here. His friends keep looking at me and him. No doubt wondering what exactly is about to happen.

Though I could punch them for not letting me know when he was going to be here. I just assumed it would be early. He never did the whole fashionably late thing. Now, I need to give him no choice but to notice me.

My feet carry me in his direction. I'm honestly in a daze seeing him after all this time. I can only hope I'm portraying the confidence I'm faking, and not the jumble of nerves I am on the inside.

This whole thing could blow up in my face. Maybe he hates me now. I don't know. The only thing I'm certain of is none of my previous relationships have worked out. Deep down, I knew they weren't him and compared every guy to the one who got away.

"Hey Jaylen," Hudson lifts his hand and waves as we get closer, "and friends." He doesn't wave to them. I swear they need to get over whatever feud they have. It's annoying at this point.

Ignoring them, I move to Patrick's side. His eyes are laser focused on the folks playing pool. I could let him keep on ignoring the fact I'm standing right in front of him, or I can use my words. "What? You aren't going to say hi?"

His throat bobs and I know I've put him on the spot. I don't care. He can't act like I don't exist. He's the one who left town and never came back. Not until now. "Hey."

One-word responses. That's where we're at now. If I'm

going to ask him to come with me to another event tomor-row, I'll need more than that. It's the only way this whole thing is going to work. It's the only way I'll be able to get him back into my life.

He doesn't seem keen to offer anything else. Small talk it is. "How have you been? Texas treating you better than Louisiana?"

"I've been good." His eyes finally move away from the pool tables, but they still don't land on me. They zero in on the beer bottle in his hands. The one he's slowly scraping the label off of with his fingernail.

Should I feel bad for putting him on the spot? Maybe. A tiny sliver of me does. But he can't act like we don't have a shared past. One full of way more great memories than bad ones.

"Just good?" Getting him to talk is almost harder than getting my students to answer a question in class. "From what I hear, the bar you work at is doing really well. I like to think you have something to do with that."

I shift my feet the tiniest bit. Trying to make any sort of movement that might get him to stop avoiding me. To acknowledge I'm here. Little does he know he's the only reason I came. Finally, his hands still around his beer bottle and his dark brown eyes lift to mine.

3

patrick

IGNORING THIS WOMAN IS IMPOSSIBLE. Always has been. I was hoping she'd walk away when I didn't engage. It seems like she's determined to torture me, though.

It's the last statement that pulls my attention from my beer. She's been checking up on me. I didn't think Jaylen cared what I did after I left. After I told her I had feelings for her and she stared at me without saying a word. I assumed she didn't care.

"Yeah, it's doing pretty well for itself." I shrug as if the recognition Out of the Ashes is getting is no big deal. It is. Especially for the small town we live in. "I'm not sure how much I have to do with it."

"You shouldn't discredit yourself." She reaches out to touch my arm, but pulls back at the last second. The act is so normal she thought nothing of it. I don't want to admit how much I wish she would have followed through.

"I'm not." Bringing the bottle to my lips, I take a drink

to give myself time to think. "People come in for the food, sure. But they also come in for the experience our bartenders give them. They know they'll get great service and drinks."

"Sounds like you have it made over there."

"It's not too bad. The heat sucks sometimes, but Asheville has the same vibe as here. Everyone knows everyone, and they are all too nosy for their own good. Especially Eric."

She takes a step closer to me. "It sounds like there is a story there."

It seems Jaylen's over the small talk, which is fine with me. But...I don't know if I want to hash all this out with her. We haven't spoken to each other in close to fifteen years. She could have easily gotten my phone number from someone if she really wanted to talk.

"Not really. Just an annoying guy who works with me and doesn't know how to mind his own business." There. That should be enough to quench her thirst for information. "Can you excuse me for a second?"

"Um, sure." She inches away from me.

I hold a finger up to my friends to let them know I'll be right back. My steps are quick as I make my way through the crowd and to the front door. Pushing it open, I breathe in the fresh air.

The sun is setting, and it's getting darker by the minute. I reach into my back pocket and pull out my phone. Talking about my annoying coworker reminded me I want to check in on them.

I scroll through my contacts for Eric's number and press call. He picks up on the third ring. "I swear if you are calling from your reunion, I'll reach through the phone and strangle you."

"I guess you better figure out how to do that, then." I clear my throat and glance behind me. Thank God, she didn't follow me out. "How's it going in the kitchen?"

"The urge to not tell you anything is strong, but I know if I don't, you'll keep calling back until I do. Which means you'll miss a good chunk of your reunion and whatever you're trying to avoid."

He's not wrong. I came out here to get a break from Jaylen. From the perfume she's wearing. From the way she looks at me, as if I actually matter when I didn't all those years ago.

"So, is it on fire? Or are you holding me in suspense?"

"Everything is fine, Patrick." Eric sighs, and I have a feeling he's shaking his head. Actually, I know he is. "Viv is working out great, and honestly, I think you should call her in more so you can take some much-needed time off."

All I'm hearing is I'm replaceable. That's not going to happen. I love working at the bar. "You're one to talk. I think you're there more than I am."

"This isn't about me," he scoffs, "besides, I'll be spreading the responsibility now that I'm with Joan."

"I'll believe it when I see it."

"I'm going to end the conversation here. I know you're eating up time, and that's weird considering I get on your nerves" he pauses for a second before continuing, "now, go enjoy yourself. You deserve it."

Before I respond, the call ends. He definitely gets on my nerves. Shoving my phone back into my pocket, I turn toward the door.

I can do this. Being around Jaylen shouldn't be this hard. It's been over a decade for crying out loud. If she can move past our fallout, so can I. It'd be easier if she didn't look so fucking beautiful in the red dress she decided to wear. It hugs her curves in all the right places.

Liam pushes the door open before I even take a step. "Hey, man, you good?"

"Yeah, I needed to check in at the bar. Had to make sure they didn't blow up my kitchen."

"Uh huh." He nods knowing damn well the reason I came out here. "And Jaylen had nothing to do with it?"

"Nope." The lie feels gross as soon as I say it. "What's up with Hudson and Kelly? I don't think I've ever seen that much hate between two people."

"You've been gone a long time and missed quite a bit. Maybe we'll fill you in when we're done here."

"Should I be afraid?"

"Not really. It's pretty funny, actually," he pulls open the door, "let's get back inside and impress our former class-mates with our accomplishments."

Rolling my eyes, I follow him inside. Taking one more deep breath, I move toward the bar. Except Jaylen isn't there anymore. Her friends are, but she's nowhere to be seen.

A flash of red moving between the crowd catches my eye and it looks like it's coming in my direction. She's deter-mined to get in my good graces tonight.

Finally, she comes into full view, and my breath catches. The same way it's done since we were teens. The way it did when I saw her walk into the bar less than an hour ago.

She's coming straight for me, and I slow my steps to gather my wits. She's less than five feet from me when she tumbles forward.

4

jaylen

ONE SECOND PATRICK is in front of me, eyes wide as I approach him for the second time tonight. The next...I'm looking up at him from his arms.

"Are you okay?" His lips are less than a foot away from mine. It would be so easy to close the distance.

But I can't. Not when I need to figure out if there can be anything between us. At least, anything more than friendship. Everything hinges on him spending more time with me.

"Hello, Jaylen." He shifts me until I'm upright, and takes a step back. My opportunity to kiss him faded away into reality. "You good? It looks like you missed a step."

"Sorry." I shake my head. "I'm not used to wearing heels."

I knew I shouldn't have let Hannah talk me into wearing these. I can count how many times I've worn heels, especially this high, since I started teaching.

She said it would make my legs look amazing and would

draw Patrick's eyes like nothing else. Little does she know, she lied. He didn't pay attention to me at all when we were talking, and then he rushed outside for some unknown reason. Honestly, I thought he was going to bail on the whole reunion.

"Not exactly great for chasing kids on the playground, huh?" So, he has kept up with me. That's good to know. Not all hope is lost.

"You'd be correct. After the first couple of years, I stopped wearing even sandals. Rocks kept getting stuck under my feet. It's not the most pleasant feeling."

Realizing what I just said, I cover my face with my hands. The last thing Patrick wants to do is hear about my feet problems while monitoring recess.

His warm hand encircles my wrists and pulls my hands away before letting go. "You don't have to be embarrassed. I've known you most of my life, and your feet have never bothered me."

It's only then I've noticed the music has softened. Not completely off, but much lower than it was five minutes ago. I can feel the eyes of our classmates on my back, and I *know* they heard the comment about my feet.

Good Lord, can tonight get any more humiliating? "Um, thanks." How the hell am I supposed to respond to that?

Moving away from him, I take a step toward the door. It's my turn to run away. There's no way in hell I'm staying in here when most of the class, at least those in our proximity, heard our exchange.

Before I can go any further, he grabs my hand, stopping me in my tracks. The gesture, so normal in our past, feels heated now. Or maybe I'm choosing to see what I want instead of what is actually happening.

He pulls me toward him. His lips are mere inches from my ear. "Don't go. Let me buy you a drink."

I wait for the music to be loud before nodding. I already know this little incident will be what everyone is talking about when we leave. Plus, there's no way I'm trusting my voice won't shake with nerves if I speak right this second.

As much as I want to march out those doors, to my car, and act like none of this happened, I can't. He's actually showing some sort of interest in talking to me, and I can't pass that up. I want, no *need*, to know the man he is now. That will tell me if I should go forward with my plan or not.

He places his hand on the small of my back. It's warm through the thin fabric of my dress, and I want nothing more than to melt into him. To close the sliver of space between us. I don't, though. He may decide to take back his offer, and I can't let that happen.

We wind through the crowd. There's no need because they part for us as if we're royalty. I have a feeling most of them knew how he felt about me way back then. Apparently, I'm the only one who was oblivious.

Even though more people have shown up, there's space for us at the bar. His friends, and mine, have spread out just far enough to make sure we can squeeze in.

I don't miss the look his friends give him. Hannah winks at me and doesn't bother trying to hide it. Please let that have slipped Patrick's notice.

"Do you still like margaritas?" he asks as he places himself between me and Liam. A small bit of separation so it feels like we're by ourselves.

"Yes, but they've gotten better at making hurricanes."

"Like the ones they serve in The Quarter?"

"Not quite, but they are still good." I grin at the disgusted look on his face. His mouth and nose scrunched as if he smelled something foul. He's never been a huge fan of the drink.

"Is that what you want?"

A quick nod is my only response. I study his profile as he turns toward the bartender and orders our drinks. There's a confidence in him I don't remember seeing when we were teens.

He's also a lot more muscular than he was back then. No longer the slim boy who avoided getting tackled on the field. I didn't let myself appreciate him the way I would have liked when I first walked in.

The bartender slides our drinks across the counter. Mine catches on a nick in the wood and leans over. Patrick catches it before it falls to its side. Good thing, too. It would have landed all over me.

"Thanks," I take the glass as he hands it to me, "that would have been a disaster."

"Sometimes I swoop in and save the day." His grin is small and reminds me so much of the boy he was when we were teens.

"So, it's still beer for you?"

"Yep." He nods toward the drink in my hand. "Let's just say I learned liquor and I didn't get along when we were teens. I don't need a repeat of those decisions. Except for the sangria one of my coworkers makes."

"Tell me more." I'm a sucker for sweet drinks. I'll talk about whatever he wants as long as we keep the conversation going.

"I honestly don't know what she puts in it. But it sneaks up on you and packs a punch. One minute you're fine and the next...not so much."

"Sounds dangerous." I try to hide my wince at the fact he's had this other woman's drinks.

But he notices. "Her boyfriend is pretty funny after he's had two. Which you wouldn't expect from a guy who sings in a band."

"Wait. You know someone in a band?" How the hell does the town he lives in have cool things there? I don't think it's much bigger than here, but it might be.

"Yeah, they play at the bar sometimes. Lately they've been opening for Crooked Halo."

"Seriously?" It's probably a good thing I don't live there. I'd be fangirling.

"Yeah, they've played at Out of the Ashes, too. It's a long-convoluted story how it all started. But they are pretty cool. And they like my food."

No wonder he doesn't come home. I wouldn't either. "That's pretty amazing." I reach out to touch his arm. This time I don't pull away. "They'd be fools not to like your food."

"Thanks," he takes a sip of his drink, "what have you been up to?"

How am I supposed to live up to everything he's just said?

5

patrick

HER EYES ARE WIDE, like a deer caught in headlights. For once, I've caught her off guard. Well, more like twice. I don't think she expected to end up in my arms when she tripped.

I hope she doesn't think I was bragging because I wasn't. The only thing I wanted to do was provide context. Her eyes got a little twitchy when I mentioned Lisa.

Unsure of what her motives are, I needed to make sure she knows I'm not currently attached to anyone. It's probably not even the case, but a guy can hope.

After a few moments, she shakes off the question. "Oh, you know, the usual. Teaching kids and meeting up here for drinks with my friends twice a week."

Another wince. This time at her own response. "Sounds pretty chill. All I do is work and go home."

I don't mention anything else I do in my spare time. It's not like I have a ton of extra time, but you can only watch so much TV without getting bored.

"And hang out with literal music stars."

"They are normal people, just like us."

She purses her lips. Clearly, she doesn't agree. "I guess."

She takes a deep breath and lets it out. And another. She must be working up the nerve to say something. This woman forgets I know her tells. Anytime she did, or said, something that made her uncomfortable she'd go through these same breathing exercises.

"You don't have to be afraid to say whatever is on your mind. I'm still the same guy."

Twenty minutes ago, I wouldn't have said that. I was ready to get in my truck and hightail it back to Asheville. But she came after me when she thought I was ditching the reunion. The least I can do is see what exactly she wants.

"How long will you be in town?" That's not the burning question I expected.

"Through the end of the week. What's up?"

It's something I haven't told the guys, or my parents. Eric told me to take longer, and for once I'm going to take his advice. Besides, they can handle the lunch crowd. Angie already told me she would close the kitchen down at night if it becomes too much.

She glances over my shoulder at her friends. A part of me wants to look back to see what they are signaling to her, but it would be too obvious.

"Well, Hannah found out about this Halloween party that's happening in New Orleans, and got us all tickets. A coworker from school was supposed to go with me, but had to cancel. Any chance you might want to take her place?"

She's lying. Not about the ticket part. But the ticket being for a friend? A quick glance down and I can see her thumb rubbing a circle into the palm of her other hand. Another quirk I've almost forgotten.

It's not something I would normally go to. Hell, I try to get out of all the special events Stella creates for the bar. Which is difficult when you're the one who runs the kitchen.

Letting Jaylen down isn't something I want to do, though. She seems dead set on going to this party, especially since the tickets are paid for.

"When is it?"

She perks up at the question. "Halloween night."

"That's in like three days." How the hell am I supposed to find a costume? Even back home, costumes in my size are hard to find. I looked because I wasn't sure I was going to come to the reunion. Stella and Angie wanted us to come to work dressed up. At least I don't have to do that now. This may be worse. I'll make an ass of myself in front of the woman standing beside me.

"I know." She holds her hands up in surrender. "If you don't want to go, it's fine. I just didn't want to go alone."

"Hannah and Kelly will be there."

She rolls her eyes and shakes her head. "You know how those two are at parties. I'm shocked they are still talking to the guys and not out on the dance floor."

Dammit, she has a point. "I don't have a costume. What if I can't find anything?"

Her face falls with each rebuttal, and I hate that I'm causing her any stress. "We can always figure something out. But, like I said, no big deal if you don't want to go."

The way her eyes shift to her feet seals the deal for me. "I'll go."

"Really?" She glances up at me through her lashes, not quite wanting to believe the agreement that fell from my lips.

"Yes, really." I can't believe I'm doing this.

"Thank you so much!" She throws her arms around my neck and hugs me, almost knocking my beer out of my hand. "You are a lifesaver."

"No problem." I wrap my arms around her waist, pulling her close to me. There isn't anything I wouldn't do to have her this close to me again. It's been so long since I've had her in my arms like this. I've missed it.

Her grip on my neck loosens, and I let her pull away from me. Her cheeks are pink, and I hope I'm the reason she's blushing.

"So, how long are y'all going to stay at this thing?" She runs her hands down her dress, smoothing it out. Little does she know it makes the fabric cling to her body. She's trying to kill me.

"I'm not sure." I glance back at the guys. "Hudson said something about going somewhere else."

"Let me guess." She taps her finger against her chin, pretending to be deep in thought. "Y'all are going to tailgate on his property."

"Good guess." It doesn't take much to come to that conclusion because that is what Hudson does. He'd rather hang out on his, or his parents', property. In his eyes, we can all crash there if we have too much to drink. More fun for us and avoiding the law. Two birds, one stone.

"At least y'all won't be roughing it in the back of the truck, or on the ground, like we used to back in the day."

"What do you mean?"

"He has a couple of RVs back there now."

Why hasn't he told me that? Maybe I should come home more often. Even though it's the same town, so many things have obviously changed.

Hudson taps my shoulder. "Hey, man, you ready to go?"

I nod a response with my focus on Jaylen. "I guess we're heading out now."

"Be careful," she leans on her toes and gives me a peck on the cheek, "do you still have my number?"

"I don't know. I've gotten a few new phones since we were in school."

She holds her hand out for my phone. Handing it over, I watch her as she quickly taps on the screen. "Here you go. I texted myself, so I have your number too."

"Good idea." I shove the phone back in my pocket. "I'll give you a call tomorrow so we can figure out the party."

"Sounds good."

The guys are already heading toward the door. "I guess I better go."

"See you later."

I give her one last hug. Anything to feel her body against mine before rushing after my friends. Being home this week will likely blow up in my face.

6

jaylen

LAST NIGHT WAS A SUCCESS. Not only did I get Patrick to open up to me, but he also agreed to go to the Halloween party. For a second, I thought he was going to say no. He gave me every excuse he could to find a way out of it.

"Are you going to coordinate costumes?" Kelly asks from the bed. She has a string of fairy lights in her hands, trying to straighten them out without tangling them. Hannah would normally be here, too, but she had to meet her parents for lunch. It's their weekly tradition.

"How are we supposed to do that?" I turn down the speaker so we can hear each other talk. "He only agreed last night, and finding a decent costume this late in the game will be nearly impossible."

"You could call and talk to him." She rolls her eyes, and looks over the supplies to finish up my costume. I had planned on having it done by now, but school has been hectic. Let's just say, I'm ready for winter break.

"Or I can wait and see what he does." Opening up a drawer in the night stand, I rummage around until I find the hot glue gun. "It was like pulling teeth for him to agree to come at all. I don't exactly want to press my luck."

"Girl, we all saw the way he was looking at you last night," she motions for the pile of tulle now that the lights are straightened out,. "He will do anything you ask of him. Even if he doesn't want to. It's always been that way with the two of you."

"No," I shake my head, "it was that way before. Now it's like neither one of us knows how to act around the other."

"Not from where we were standing." She laughs. "The way he caught you when you tripped...it was like a moment out of a movie."

"I'm glad my tripping in heels made you swoon." Maybe we should lay off watching rom-coms for a while. "This is whole new territory for me. Back then we were best friends. I went to him for everything. Then he dropped the feelings bomb on me and I didn't react the way I should have. Now...I don't know that we'll ever get that back."

"Do you want to be just friends with him?" She glances up at me while hot gluing the fairy lights to my tulle skirt. "Or, do you want more?"

"Obviously I want more." Her asking that question is asinine. It's the whole reason we devised this whole plan to begin with. To get him to have some alone time with me. For us to get to know each other again.

"Then you'll have to take risks." She continues putting my skirt together, and doesn't look at me. "Don't be that scared girl you were in high school. You took the easy route back then to keep from getting hurt. Now it's time to put it all on the line."

She hit the nail on the head. I was scared back then. I loved him so much. He was the one I went to for everything. If I'm being honest with myself, I wanted him as more than a best friend in high school, but the timing never felt right. And when he finally told me he had feelings for me one drunken night, I chose the safe route. He wanted to leave our town and go into the big scary world. I stayed closed and lived out the life I had mapped out for myself.

"How am I supposed to do that?" My life is so predictable, I don't know if I remember how to live outside the lines.

"First off," she lifts the tulle, "you should have chosen a costume that's not so sweet and innocent."

"You know I can't go out in anything considered scandalous. If photos ever get out, I could lose my job." Being an angel with lights and a shorter tulle skirt seems like a pretty safe bet.

"You realize most of the costumes are going to be scary, right? You'll stick out like a sore thumb."

"What are you and Hannah dressing up as?" They've been very tight-lipped about their costumes, and it's honestly weird.

"You'll just have to wait and see." Ugh, they are supposed to be my best friends. But I also know they are the horror buffs in our trio. I'm the one who has to watch happy cartoons after I watch a scary movie with them.

"I guess." Rolling my eyes, I pull out the bag of white feathers Kelly told me to get. "Are we going to need these?" It feels like a lot, but Kelly's been making her own costumes since we were kids. I trust her judgment.

"Definitely." She winces as a piece of the hot glue catches her on the finger. "It'll hide the wire around the skirt and the light will peek through."

You'd think being an elementary teacher, I'd be the super creative one in the group, but I'm not. I have to scour the internet for any ideas on projects to do with my students. Kelly usually gives me ideas as well.

"Okay. Do you want me to find you some gardening gloves so you don't burn yourself with the glue gun again?"

"Nope, I've got this." She works the wire through the skirt and glues another piece down. "Do you know what shoes you're wearing, or how you're doing your hair and makeup?"

"Um, sort of." She's not going to like my answer, I can already feel it. "I have a pair of white high tops to wear, and haven't completely decided on the hair or makeup. I just know I'm adding sparkles."

Kelly's hands come to a halt, and she sets the glue gun down on the plate sitting on my nightstand. "The sparkles are fine for both hair and makeup. It'll add to the sweet and innocent look. But the high tops...not happening. I know the heels last night were a chore, but they made your legs look amazing in that dress. It'll do the same for this costume. I literally just told you to stop being so safe in your choices."

"But I'll trip over my own feet again if I wear heels. Besides, I don't have any white ones." I really don't want to wear those torture devices again. Even when we all went to prom in high school, I wore a dress long enough to cover the flip flops I wore.

"I've got you covered." She grins and goes back to gluing on the lights. "And you're not going to fall because you'll have Patrick by your side. He'll be there to save you from your clumsiness just like he did last night."

"I'm not sure if you're a mad genius, or watch too many movies." Honestly, it could be a bit of both.

"Definitely genius," she laughs, "can you separate the feathers into piles of short & long? I'll need to vary them when I add them."

"Sure." One thing about Kelly, she's very detail oriented. But I think that works in my favor. Now I just have to get through a couple of days of teaching before I have my chance with Patrick.

My phone rings, and both of us look at the screen. Patrick's name flashes across and I hope like hell he's not backing out.

7

patrick

MY OPTIONS ARE LIMITED. Why did I agree to go to this thing with Jaylen? Three stores, and I can't find anything that's not completely cheesy. It'd be great if I could find a costume, I'm remotely interested in wearing since I'll probably take it home with me for whatever events Out of the Ashes may do in the future. But, no such luck. I'll have to resort to finding something in my dad's closet and the fit won't be great.

"Dude, why are you so stressed about this?" Hudson shakes his head at me from the passenger seat. "It's a party, and not that serious."

Except it is. It feels like Jaylen and I are starting over, and I don't want to ruin that. I think she wants more than friendship, but I'm going to let her lead the way. If she doesn't, then I'll be happy to be in her life as a friend. There are so many times I've wanted to pick up the phone and call her to tell her what's going on in my life, and to hear what she's been up to. But I couldn't because I ruined it after one drunken night before graduation.

"I'm not stressed."

"You get more and more agitated with each store we walk out of."

He's not wrong, but I don't need him to point it out. "I just want to make sure I have an actual costume."

"Then call her and see what she's dressing up as," He shakes his head. "Then you can match or whatever."

"Are you sure you're not mad you weren't invited?"

"No," he grunts. "Do you have any idea how terrible traffic is going to be?"

I haven't, and while it's not my favorite thing, I'll deal with it for Jaylen. "I can always send you pictures so you'll feel like you're there."

"I'd rather you not." He stares out the window as I drive through town. "Actually, do you want to drop me off at the house? I think I'm still hungover."

There's no thinking, he's definitely still hungover. There's a reason I don't drink as much as I did in high school. And why I don't drink liquor. That's the whole reason I lost my friendship with Jaylen to begin with. I got drunk, in my feelings, and told her I loved her as more than a friend.

"Sure. Do you need anything before I drop you off?"

"Nope. I have everything I need at home."

"Okay." I turn down the main road out of town that will lead me to Hudson's house.

* * *

Hudson is at his house, and I'm at a loss as to what to do with the rest of my day. I had originally planned on leaving today. In just a few hours I would be closing in on home. But no, I'm still here, doing whatever the girl I loved asks of me.

Speaking of, Hudson wasn't wrong about needing to call her. It'll help with costume coordination because I have no idea which direction to take it.

I don't want to go home in case I need to go back to the store. There aren't as many people on the road as I'd expect today. I guess everyone is still sleeping off their hangovers from the reunion last night. I pull into a gas station and put the truck in park so I'm not on the phone while driving.

I grab my phone off the dashboard and look for her information she put in. I press the call icon when I get to her name. The phone rings once, twice, three times, before she picks up.

"Hello?" She sounds different today. Like she's panicked.

"Hey, Jaylen." I wait for her to say anything else, but she doesn't. "Are you okay?"

"Oh, yeah, sorry. Me and Kelly are working on my costume for the Halloween party."

"Good. That's actually what I want to talk to you about."

"Oh yeah?" She pauses for a second. "Are you having second thoughts about going?"

"No, not at all. I told you I would go with you, and I will."

"Okay. What do you need?"

"What does your costume look like? I'm trying my luck at the stores today and it might help if I had something in mind to look for."

"Um, hold on." I hear her hand cover the phone and

muffled voices talk in the background. Too bad I can't make out what they are saying. After a couple of minutes she comes back online. "You still there?"

"Yeah," I draw out. I don't know if I should be scared or not.

"Soooo, I'm not going to tell you what I'm dressing as," her voice is shaky with the words as if she's not convinced, she should be saying them. "Kelly and I both agree you should be surprised when you pick me up for the party."

Huh. I didn't realize I was picking her up, but it makes sense. At least she also sees this as a date, and not just a random friend outing. That makes me feel slightly better about being nervous for the party.

"How am I supposed to know what to be if I don't know what you are?"

"Surprise me." I can hear the smile in her voice now. The playful woman coming to the forefront. "It doesn't have to be anything elaborate. It's not like I gave you a ton of notice for the party."

Or any at all. "Okay." I relent. "I don't know how amazing it will be."

"As long as it's a costume, you'll be fine."

"I can't just show up?"

"Nope. Costumes are mandatory per the party rules." Of course, they are. This definitely feels like something Stella would put on at the bar. Actually, I wouldn't be surprised if she's doing that very thing as we speak.

"I'll see what I can come up with." I don't know what else to say to her, and she's with Kelly. As much as I'm cool with her friends, I don't like being on the phone when they are all around. "I need to get back to the house. Talk to you later?"

"Yeah," she pauses for a second, "bye, Patrick."

"See you later, Jay."

With that, I disconnect the call. I guess I need to search through all the closets at home and see what I can throw together. Hopefully it's enough.

8

jaylen

TONIGHT, is the night. The work day felt like it took forever to end. Not only am I anxious because of my date tonight. I refuse to see it as anything else. But the kids were amped up about going out and getting candy.

Patrick and I have talked to each other on the phone the past couple of days when I get home from work. Honestly, I feel a little bad he has to listen to me vent about the school day. He hasn't complained about it once. In a lot of ways, it feels like that connection we had all those years ago is back. I know I can go to him with anything and there will be no judgment.

I didn't want to call him today, though. My girls are needed, even though I'll see them in a few hours. Both of them decided not to get ready at my place. Which sucks because I could really use their help.

Kelly and Hannah are on the phone with me as I get ready. I tried to get them to hop on a video call so they could make sure I didn't look ridiculous, but they were serious about me not seeing their costumes. I'm going to be mad if it isn't epic.

"How does everything fit?" Kelly asks. I can hear Hannah singing, badly, in the background. If I didn't know better, I'd say she's already tipsy.

"Okay, I think."

"What do you mean, you think?"

"I have no idea how I'm going to get the wings on by myself." We tried them on when Kelly was here last weekend to make sure they felt alright, but it took both of us to get them on.

"You don't need them yet."

"Why not?"

"Because you still have to get in his truck to drive to Generations Hall." She sighs, "as spacious as I'm sure his truck is, I don't think it's big enough for your wings to be on your body and not get smashed at the same time."

"You have a point."

"How's the hair and makeup?"

All these questions could have been avoided if they were here or if we were on video. "Both look okay."

"Send me a pic." I don't hear Hannah in the background anymore. There's no telling where she disappeared to. Possibly to get another drink.

Picking up my phone, I open the camera, snap a selfie and send it to her. Crap, my battery is getting lower and lower. I pull the cord from the side of my dresser and plug it into my phone before I prop it up again.

"Did you get it?" I don't like the silence coming from the other end. I'm not sure if it's good or bad.

"Yep. Add a little more glitter to your cheekbones and you're good to go."

"Thank God." I grab the body glitter from the dresser and tap it with my finger. "I was worried it was horrible."

"You look amazing! Patrick isn't going to know what hit him."

"Yeah," Hannah calls from the back. "You're gonna have him eating from the palm of your hands."

"Please tell me you're the one driving, Kelly."

"I am. I knew she was going to pregame, I even booked us two rooms at a nearby hotel."

"You didn't have to do that." She really is too kind for her own good.

"I know." I can hear the smile in her voice, "but I wanted this night to be perfect for you. I even talked to Hudson and he snuck an overnight bag into Patrick's truck. Check the closet and you'll find yours."

I know talking to Hudson probably wasn't the greatest for her. The animosity between those two is ridiculous, but as long as it doesn't screw up my night, I'll be fine. "Thank you."

There's a knock at the front door and I panic. "Oh my God, he's here."

"First, calm down," Kelly laughs, "then hang up with me and answer the door."

"I need to turn on my lights."

"No, wait until you get there. Have him help you put on the wings, then turn on the lights. Wait to give him the full effect."

My thoughts run through my mental to-do list. Costume. Check. Hair and makeup. Check. Bag for hotel. Check. Tickets... "Crap, I forgot to get our tickets from you."

"Don't worry, we'll be there at the same time."

"But I don't know what you're dressed as." They just had to make everything difficult.

"You'll see us." Hannah's words are slurred. There's no way she's making it through the whole party before leaving or getting kicked out.

"Okay. But if I don't recognize you, you know what my costume looks like."

"Yes," both of them say in unison. Kelly adds, "now go get the door before Patrick thinks he has the wrong house."

"Okay, okay." I groan as I turn toward the bed, making sure all of the accessories are together. "I'll see y'all there."

Ending the call, I rush over to the closet and pull out the bag Kelly left me. Setting it next to the wings, I take a deep breath. My steps are quick but sure as I head to the front door. I don't have the heels on yet. I'm waiting as long as possible before I put on those torture devices. My phone dings with a text as my hand reaches for the knob. I pull it from the pocket Kelly added to the skirt. How? I don't know. She's magical that way.

Patrick: I'm here. I think. The door hasn't been answered and I've been knocking for a bit.

It's about time I answer the door. If I don't, he's going to leave, and he may not come back. There's no way in hell I'm going to let that happen. Not after I put in all this work. Deep breath in, and out. I repeat that two more times before wrapping my hand around the knob and opening the door.

Patrick is a dark shadow in front of the setting sun. Before I have a chance to say hello, he lifts a hand to his chest as if it hurts. "You look stunning."

"Just wait until you see it all put together." I take a step back and motion my hand towards inside. "Please, come in."

9

patrick

I KEEP GLANCING over at Jaylen. Stunning doesn't cover how amazing she looks. She said she chose an angel because there's no way it can be misconstrued as something bad if pictures get out of the party. Which I'm assuming they will for marketing purposes. The fact she could potentially get fired for going out is terrifying, and kudos to her for thinking things through.

"Did you know we were going to have a room prior to tonight?"

Jaylen glances over at me and shakes her head. "I found out about five minutes before you picked me up. My friends like to keep me on my toes."

"Sounds like it," I chuckle softly, "the fact that Hudson knew is mind boggling to me. Or that he actually packed some clothes for me and put them in the backseat."

"I'm sure Kelly threatened something horrible if he didn't." She laughs, still shaking her head. "She can be... persuasive."

"I have no doubt about that." Back in high school, she could put the fear of God in anybody. Including me. I remember when she told me I had to buy a certain color flower for her wrist. She even gave me pictures and told me which florist to go to.

Slowly, I inch the truck forward as the car line moves. I'm not sure what to say to Jaylen. The pressure has been building up all week to this moment. It's just the two of us in my truck, and I feel like that rambling teenager who told her he loved her.

Finally, we make it to the front of the line. A person with half their face painted like a skeleton opens the door. This event really went all out. Maybe I should be taking notes for Stella. Another person on the staff opens the door for Jaylen. She turns toward the backseat, but I wave her off. "I've got these."

"Thanks." She closes the door and comes around the truck. With her wings in one hand, I give my information to the valet driver and he hands me a ticket.

"When you're ready, just bring us the ticket and we'll get your vehicle for you."

Nodding my agreement, I turn toward Jaylen. "Are you ready to go in?"

"Um, actually, we have to wait for Hannah and Kelly to get here. They have our tickets."

"Oh." I wish I'd known that. We wouldn't have left her house so early. "Maybe we should move over here to the side so we're not in anyone's way."

"That's a good idea," she moves outside of the entrance, and I follow her. Let's be honest, I'd follow this woman pretty much anywhere. "Can you help me with the wings while we wait? It's a two-person job."

"Of course."

She turns around, facing the wall and holds her arms out to the side. The wings are bulky, and I slide an arm loop around both arms at the same time. It's probably easier to do it this way than to bend her arms at odd angles to get the wings adjusted. Once I'm sure they won't slide down, I move in front of her and move the wings further up her arms.

My fingers glide slowly across her skin with the movement, and I'm pretty sure she just shuddered at the touch. Taking a step closer to her, I adjust the straps of material. Untwisting them so they lay flat across her shoulders. This is the closest I've been to her since the reunion. I move my hand to her cheek, my thumb caressing her glitter covered skin.

"You look beautiful." I haven't even seen the full effect of the costume, but I know without a doubt she's going to outshine everyone there.

"Th-thanks." Her breath catches on the words. On this crowded street, with people waiting to get into the event, it feels like it's only the two of us here. Everyone else fades away. A replay of the night I told her how I felt about her, but this time...this time she's on the same page as me.

I close the distance between us, her body flush against mine. My lips are a mere inch from hers. Her eyes close and suddenly there's light shining from above us. "There you go."

Pulling back, I glance over Jaylen's shoulder. Kelly and Hannah are standing behind her beaming. Jaylen groans as she turns around, and I have to shuffle to the side to avoid her wings. "Seriously."

"I added lights to the halo as well. You're welcome."

With their appearance, the moment is ruined. "Uh, thanks." I watch Jaylen eye her best friends. "Y'all really didn't think I'd like to dress up as my childhood favorite doll?"

"We knew you might have other plans." Hannah blurts out and covers her mouth. So, they orchestrated this whole thing. How many people knew? Is that why my friends were constantly bugging me about coming to the reunion? No, they don't even talk to Hannah and Kelly if they don't have to.

"Speaking of," Kelly turns toward me, "what are you supposed to be?"

My back stiffens now that the attention is on me. "Um, a cowboy."

Kelly opens the small bag looped over her shoulder. She pulls out a few things and draws on my face. "There, now you're an injured cowboy." She slides the makeup back into her bag. "You can't show up in the same thing you used to wear in school."

"It's the best I could do with short notice."

"I know, and I made it slightly better." She grins. "Jaylen is the angel sent to help you on your way."

Out of the corner of my eye, I watch Jaylen shake her head. I think she's as exasperated with her friends as I am. "Do you have our tickets?"

"Yep." She pulls two small rectangles, and a key card, out of her bag and hands them to the woman beside me before leaning in and whispering something in her ear. She steps back and waves at us. "You two have fun, and definitely do everything we would do." With that they turn around and leave.

Jaylen's cheeks are bright red. "You, okay?"

"Absolutely," she grins up at me, "let's get in line to go in."

"Let's do this." I take a deep breath and hold out my

hand. This whole thing is so far outside of my comfort zone, I don't know what to do with myself.

"Hold on." She pushes some of the fabric away, pushes something, and her entire skirt lights up. I didn't even realize there were lights on it. They shine through the feathers, making her literally glow. "Now I'm ready."

"Yep, definitely out of this world." She grabs my hand and we move toward the line of people waiting to get in. "If we get separated, I'll be able to find you."

"I guess it's a good thing I don't plan on leaving your side tonight."

"Any chance you want to fill me in on what Kelly said?"

She doesn't answer right away, and I observe the people in line in front of us. There are two guys talking to each other. One is wearing a long coat with a cape. He has a pipe held in one hand as he talks and a cap on top of his head. The other man is wearing a bowler hat with a navy coat, and I think a fake mustache. It could be real, but I doubt it. I rack my brain trying to figure out where I've seen those characters before.

"Not a chance." Jaylen finally answers. She nods to the men in front of us, and adds, "but if you really want to know, I'm sure Sherlock and Watson could puzzle it out."

10

jaylen

THE PARTY just started and there are already people milling about inside. I think this is the first time I've seen people arrive on time for an event. Most of the time, fashionably late is the standard. I guess with an event like this, people want to soak up as much fun as they can.

Patrick's eyes are wide as he takes in the venue. I've been here for a few concerts, but I've never seen it decked out quite like this. I bump into his arm. "So, what do you want to do first?"

"A drink." He nods toward one of the bars, "definitely a drink."

His hand grips mine as we weave through the crowd. The line at the bar isn't too bad since it looks like they have multiple bars throughout the space. This isn't even all of it. I can't wait to see what else they have set up for us to explore.

There is a menu sitting on top of the bar when we make

our way to the front. "It doesn't look like they have anything either of us drink. Do you know what you want?"

He glances over the menu and scrunches up his nose. Everything includes liquor, and he made it pretty clear he doesn't drink it often the other night. I wonder if he'll go with water instead. "Not yet, do you have a preference?"

I tap my finger on my chin, trying to decide so I don't hold up the line. There's only one drink that includes rum. "Let's go with Lucifer's Demon."

Patrick laughs loud, causing a few people around us to jump. "You realize why that's funny, right?"

"Nooo." It's a drink. Why in the world would it be funny.

"What are you dressed as?" He waves his hand in front of me, "and what's the name of the drink?"

"Oh my God." Now, I'm the one laughing. He's right. It's funny. "I wonder if it's as sinful as the name implies?"

"There's only one way to find out." He waves at one of the bartenders and they come over. "Can I get a Lucifer's Demon and a...Red Rum?"

So, he is going to drink tonight. Let's hope he handles it better than he did when we were teens. The only difference between now and then? I'm fully capable of speaking up for myself and letting him know that I do in fact want him as more than a best friend. Even if we're only getting back into the friendship groove, I want, no need him as more than that. I have for years.

The bartender slides our drinks across the bar and Patrick hands him a couple of bills, motioning for him to keep the change. We grab our drinks and Patrick reaches for my hand again. Sliding mine into his, I can't help the gut feeling I have that this is right. This is how it should be, and how we should have been all these years if I wasn't such an idiot as a teenager.

Patrick leads us to a secluded section to the side of the dance floor. We watch the party goers having the time of their lives for a few minutes before he turns to me. "I think I'm glad I came tonight."

"You think? What else would you be doing tonight if you weren't here?" I have to yell to be heard over the music. His answer will let me know a little more about who he is now. Also, if he has any hobbies outside of work.

"Probably doing something similar. But I'd be on the side of the staff instead of an attendee." So, he'd be working. "My boss has started doing events like this at the bar for holidays. I think she's even planning on doing some sort of cupid thing for Valentine's Day. It seems pointless to me, but themed events bring in more business."

"That sounds like a lot." I can't imagine this mostly shy man mingling with people at these events. We're the same when it comes to large crowds of people, especially ones we don't know. If it wasn't for Hannah and Kelly, I wouldn't be here. "How do you handle it?"

"Easy, I stay in the kitchen." He grins down at me, and I'm glad he has an area he can get away. "The crowds aren't horrible when we have the events. It's mostly our regulars and a few folks from surrounding cities stop by to see what the bar is all about. But I'm usually busy with whatever themed food they've planned."

"How do y'all keep the bar open and do these events?"

"When we do them, we only have the bar open for the ticketed event. It's closed to the general public. But we make enough off of the events to keep doing them. At least, I assume we do. Otherwise, I don't think Angie and Carlos would keep doing them."

"At least the crowd isn't the size of this." I gesture with my drink to the people surrounding us.

"Not even close. Thank God." He looks down at my costume and the smile that crosses his face warms my entire body. "You're the brightest person in this room." He holds his drink toward me, and I clink mine with his. "Thank you for inviting me."

Honestly, if he hadn't agreed to come, I wouldn't be here. As much as I love my friends, this isn't my scene. I'd be at home curled up with a glass of wine watching a show I've seen a million times before.

"Thank you for coming." The yelling is getting hard to handle with some many people around. "Do you want to check out what else they have in the other rooms?"

"What?" He leans down until his ear is close to my mouth, and I wish he'd turn. I'm still mad Kelly interrupted what would have been our first kiss before we came in. A small part of me wonders if she did it on purpose. Most likely. She's the queen of building suspense, and her butting in would do just that.

"I said, do you want to check out the rest of the event? I'm sure they have other things happening besides dancing."

"Sure." He releases my hand, and slides it to the small of my back. The gesture is possessive and sweet at the same time. "Lead the way."

My eyes bounce around the area until I find an opening. Even though I wish my hand was still in his, I'm glad he's still touching me. I move forward and other guests of the party close in around us. He moves his hand from my back to around my waist. His fingers softly gripping my side to ensure we don't get separated. I can't help but wonder what that would feel like without the fabric between us.

11

patrick

APPARENTLY, everyone else found the same opening Jaylen did because the crowd around us swells as they try to get to the dance floor. My grip on her tightens and she pauses until her back is against my chest. She reaches back with her free hand, feeling her way around my waist until she slides a finger through the loop on my jeans.

Right now, I wish we were anywhere but here. Somewhere we could be alone. We could talk and figure out where exactly we stand. I can't leave this town without knowing what is happening between us. I'm also not moving back home. I love living in Asheville, and my job. Could we make long distance work? If we figure out what we are, we can make decisions regarding our future.

I knew the second I saw her I would be pulled back into her orbit. Pulled back into her being my everything, just like she was all those years ago.

We move through the crowd, working our way around the dance floor until we find a staircase. It's not roped off, and there isn't a bouncer around. Jaylen takes the steps slowly and I follow behind her in case she loses her balance. After the fall the other night at the reunion, I'm surprised she chose heels again. Though, if I had to guess, her friends forced her into it. One of these days she'll stand up to them. But I have a feeling she'll yank them off as soon as we leave.

"I think up here will be better." She yells. There isn't a need since it's less crowded up here. The perfect spot to catch your breath and take a break from the crowd. I glance around the layout, checking out the space. There's even a bar up here. Maybe we don't have to go back down at all.

She releases my belt loop and walks in front of me, using the glow from her skirt to light the way. "There's a free table over there." I point to the end of the walkway we're currently on. We definitely weren't the only ones with the same idea.

Jaylen picks up her pace and I follow behind her. Another couple is making their way to the same table, and she's determined we get to it first. The only thing we have on our side is our proximity. She reaches the table before I do, and leans on it, claiming it.

I catch up and pull a chair out for her. She collapses into it. Considering she's dressed like an angel, grace is not her strong suit. "We've barely been here an hour and these shoes are already killing me."

It's easier to hear her, and I don't feel the need to yell as I sit opposite of her. "You could have worn regular shoes."

"I know." She waves my comment away. "But apparently these make my legs look amazing."

They absolutely do. She's always had curves, and muscular legs. All the years we played chicken in the pool as teens can attest to that. I don't think there was a worse form of torture than having the girl I loved legs wrapped around my shoulders. Hudson used to think I had the patience of a saint.

"They look great no matter what you're wearing." My mouth closes shut as soon as the words are out of my mouth. Way to sound creepy, Patrick.

"Thanks." She's looking at the table as she spins her drink in her hands, but I can see the way her lips tilt up at the compliment.

Glancing over the railing, I take in the view. We can see everything happening on the first floor. People grinding on each other. From this vantage point it doesn't look as crowded as it felt being in the midst of it. "I think I see Kelly and Hannah."

I point to the dance floor, and what I think they were wearing when we saw them before we came in. They aren't alone. Both of them have gentlemen grinding against them to the music. It's always amazed me how Jaylen is friends with them. They like to be the center of attention while Jaylen watches from the sidelines. Though, I guess the same could be said of me and my friends. It's probably why I loved spending so much time with the woman in front of me. She was my safe space. Where I felt comfortable being myself and not putting on a facade when we went out.

"That didn't take them long." She laughs and shakes her head.

"What do you mean?"

"For them to find guys." She waves in their direction. "It's always been easy for them to find someone."

"If I remember correctly, it wasn't that difficult for you when we were in high school." I remember back to all the times she would animatedly tell me about the dates she went on. Not that I stayed single in hopes of her dating me. But I kept most girls at arm's length, and it was something they always commented on. They knew I wasn't really into relationships.

"It's not like they were great boyfriends." She sighs and takes a drink. "You'll also remember I used to call you crying when one of them inevitably broke my heart, or did something stupid."

She's not wrong. I did come to her defense on more than one occasion. Most of the guys she dated were also jealous of our friendship. They didn't want her to have anything to do with me when they were together, and both of us were too stubborn to care. Nothing was going to come between our friendship. Until I did it myself.

"Speaking of, I'm surprised you haven't found your happily ever after. Guys would be stupid not to hang onto you when they get the chance."

She takes a long sip of her drink, buying herself time to respond. I can't blame her since I put her on the spot. Not by accident, either. I need to know if I stand a chance with her. Being with her tonight should be enough of an answer, but it isn't. Unlike fifteen years ago, I need to hear the words from her lips.

"I've dated a few people. Some from the district, and some I've met while hanging out with Kelly and Hannah," she takes another drink. "But nothing came from it. We didn't have anything in common, and none of them compare—"

She cuts off her words, not wanting to finish the sentence. Not wanting to admit what we've both no doubt done throughout the years. Pushed people away because they weren't the person we truly wanted.

"Compared to what?" Am I being pushy by asking her to finish the statement? Probably. Do I care? Not really, because I want to hear her say it. I want her to say that even back then, I was the person she wanted even if she couldn't admit it then.

She lifts her glass to her lips, only to realize there's nothing in it. She stands and takes a step toward the bar, but I place a hand over hers. "Jaylen?"

"Fine." She throws her hands up in the air. She's not exactly angry, though bystanders may think differently. She sits back down and studies the table top. "They weren't you, Patrick. Not a single person I ever dated measured up to you."

12

jaylen

I. AM. Mortified. There was no way to get around the conversation without admitting the one thing I refused to voice aloud. Even my friends knew the reason, but they never asked for confirmation. But Patrick wasn't relenting until I told him. Now, it's out there, and he hasn't said a single word.

His eyes are trained on me, I can feel them studying me. The chair he's sitting in shifts, and before I have a chance to react, he's kneeling on the floor beside me. Oh God. What is he doing?

He places his thumb on my chin and lifts my face until I'm staring into his dark brown eyes. "That's all I needed to know."

Without pause, his lips crash into mine. The sweet, tender boy I've known my entire life is gone. Replaced by the man in front of me, claiming me with his mouth and tongue. His hands tangled in my hair as he takes what I've known he's wanted for the better part of our lives.

My hands move to the front of his shirt, gripping the fabric. Holding him to me so he doesn't drift away once again. Our tongues dance as he deepens the kiss. The moment I didn't realize until recently I wanted is perfect. Well, almost.

Cheering and whoops fill the space around us, and I remember we are very much in public. My entire body flushes as the realization hits, and I slowly pull away from him. He leans his forehead against mine, breaths quick, as he calms down.

"You have no idea how long I've wanted to do that," he chuckles, "just so you know, it's been the same for me. Every woman I've ever dated, trying to forget you, never held a candle to you."

"At least I know I'm unforgettable." Part of me is hurt he tried to forget me. But I can't blame him. I never gave him a reason to reach out to me. To try anything with me.

That one drunken night before we graduated, he professed his love for me. Told me if I gave him a chance, he'd stay. He'd find a culinary school closer to home to be with me. I couldn't let him do that. He was going to the school he dreamed of. Holding him back would do nothing for him. At the time I didn't realize I felt anything more than friendship for him. So, I stayed silent. Let him think the worst, and he left as soon as he could without a goodbye.

"There was never any doubt about that." He grins.

"Can you, um, get up?" I glance around at the crowd gathering close to us. "These folks probably think we just got engaged or something."

He moves off his knees, picks up his cowboy hat that fell, and sits across from me. "Sorry." He ducks his head.

There's the shy guy I love. "I didn't know how else to get your attention."

"You definitely got it." I lift my drink before remembering it's empty. "Can you get me another one of these?"

"Sure thing." He stands and bends down to kiss my temple. "I'll be right back."

Fanning myself with my hands, I try to cool down. It's not that hot up here, but my body is on fire. I slide his drink toward me, there's nothing left but watered-down ice and I take a sip to help. It does absolutely nothing.

A woman dressed as a pirate stops by our table and bends down. "Congratulations. It's always been my dream to get engaged on Halloween. It's my favorite holiday."

"N-no, we're not—" Before I have a chance to explain she walks away. I have a feeling this is going to be the talk of the party, and nothing even happened. Well, other than the mind shattering kiss I just shared with Patrick. If he can make me melt with only a kiss, I can't imagine how it's going to feel when we fall into bed together. Who knows, maybe I'll get to find out tonight.

"What was that about?" Patrick sets my drink in front of me. I expect him to sit across from me again, but he moves the chair over until he's beside me. He sits down and his free hand automatically goes to my knee. The reserved touches from earlier are no longer necessary. Not now that he knows I want him as much as he wants me.

"Oh, you know, just some random stranger congratulating me on our upcoming nuptials." I shake my head and laugh because it's all I can do at this point. The one time I'm the center of attention, it's because I got my first kiss with my childhood best friend.

"My bad." He doesn't look sorry at all. The wide grin he's sporting as he watches the people still staring at us says he's pretty proud of himself. I don't blame him, though. He never would have had the confidence to do that at eighteen. Now, in our mid-thirties, he's sure of what he wants. Even if that person lives hours away from him, and has no idea how we are going to make this work.

"It's all good." I lean my head on his shoulder. "I'd say it was more than worth it."

We sit in silence as the DJ continues to play music downstairs. There are still a couple of hours until this thing ends. And as much as I want to ditch the rest of the party and head straight to our hotel room, I know we should stay a little longer. Especially since our tickets were essentially free. I know the payoff will be fine with Kelly, though. This was her moment to play fairy godmother. Her way of making my wildest dreams come true.

"Want to see what else this party has to offer?" Patrick squeezes my knee. It might be my imagination, but I think his hand moved further up my leg. There's a good chance he's having the same thoughts I am. Both of us are too polite to voice them aloud.

"Sure." I stand and he does the same. Grabbing my drink, I hook a finger into his belt loop. Not so accidentally grabbing his butt in the process.

"You keep doing that and I'll carry you out of here."

The drinks are working their way through my system because what falls from my lips next is something I'd never say. "Don't make promises you can't keep."

13

patrick

DID she just say what I think she did? I almost ask her to repeat it, but if she does, there's no way in hell we're staying here a second longer. More people from downstairs are finding their way to the balcony, and I position myself closer to Jaylen. Bending down, I whisper in her ear, "it's a promise I intend to keep."

The small gasp that falls from her lips is exactly the reaction I was hoping for. I wrap my arm around her shoulder as we make our way to the stairs. We descend slowly so her heel doesn't catch, and if we come up or down the stairs again, I'm carrying her. There's no reason she should torture her feet to look good for me.

"Where do we want to go? I think there are two other rooms." She looks around the space, trying to figure out what direction to take.

"Let's walk around and see where we end up." There really aren't that many people here. Definitely less than three hundred. Now that more folks have showed up, I study all their costumes, and feel underdressed. This feels like a party for the elite, and I can't imagine how much tickets cost. There's no way Jaylen could afford them on a teacher's salary. I don't want to bring it up, though. Maybe she saved up for these tickets in hopes I would come. She put a lot of faith in me saying yes.

Jaylen moves in the direction we came from when we first got here, except she's not going to the other side of the dance floor. There's a door directly in the back, and I follow her through it. The space isn't as big as the main room. The vibe is cozier and the dance floor is half the size.

There's a raised platform off to the side and a woman is sitting at a table in the corner. A glass ball in front of her on a pedestal. Another woman sits in front of her, attention focused solely on the woman with the cards.

"I didn't know they were going to have fortune tellers. That's so fun." Jaylen moves her hand from my waist and takes a step forward. "I wonder how much it is." She takes a step closer to the raised platform and sees a sign. VIP ONLY. Her face falls, and I hate that she's disappointed.

I wish more than anything I could get her up there to participate, but I don't even know where to get a pass for that. "Maybe I can find out where to get a pass."

"No, no, it's fine." It's not. She really wants to do it, even though both of us know it's not real. It's a fun thing to do, especially on Halloween. "Can you hold this for a second?" She points toward the other side of the room. "I need to go to the restroom."

"Absolutely." I grab her drink. "I'll be here when you get back."

I wait until she's lost in the crowd and head over to the closest bar. When one of the bartenders is free, I wave her over. "Do you know where I can get a VIP pass for the fortune teller?"

"They came with the VIP passes." She points to a person wearing a wristband. "I don't think there's another way to get them."

"Dang it." I shake my head. "I need to find a way to get one. The girl I've loved for basically my entire life really wants to see the fortune teller, and I want to make that happen for her."

"I'm sorry, Sir. I can keep an ear out to see if anyone is leaving and doesn't want it anymore."

"That would be great, thank you." It's a long shot, I know that. But for once, I need luck on my side. Now that I know she feels the same way about me, hell even if she didn't, I want to make sure tonight is perfect for her.

I'm not sure how long Jaylen will be in the restroom so I make my way back to the area by the fortune teller to wait for her. Luckily, nobody else has taken the spot. I keep searching for her bright dress, but I don't see it yet. Hopefully, she's okay.

I'm about to go look for her when someone steps in front of me. "Hi, my friend and I heard you talking to the bartender."

Was I that loud? I didn't mean for anyone but the bartender to overhear me. "Oh, um, hi."

"He's the one dressed up like Cousin Itt." She waves him off, "anyway, he has no interest in seeing the fortune teller, and wants you to have this."

She hands me a wristband exactly like the one the bartender pointed out. "Th-thank you."

"No problem." She waves away my words. "I know things like that are silly, but I hope this helps you make her night magical."

"You have no idea." I grip the wristband in my hand. "I wish there was some way I could repay you."

"Don't worry about it. Halloween is a fun night, and I know she'll appreciate it." Before I can say anything else, she walks back toward the guy with long hair covering him from head to toe. How did I miss that guy when I was over there? Too bad Jaylen is in the restroom and misses it.

I'm watching the woman and Cousin Itt walk away when someone wraps an arm around my waist. "Who was that?"

"Just someone who wanted you to have something."

"What?" She looks around curiously. "I don't even know that person. Are you sure it's something I'll want."

"Positive." I hand her the drink she gave me, and grab her hand, sliding the band over her wrist. "Looks like the Gods are smiling down on you tonight."

"Wh-what is this?" I take her hand and lead her around the railing to entrance onto the platform.

"Your VIP pass," I grin down at her, "you get to see the fortune teller after all."

14

jaylen

"PLEASE TELL me you didn't spend a small fortune on this." I'm grateful he went out of his way to get one for me, but I knew going in what this party was for. It's a networking event, and we only managed to get in because of the connections Hannah and Kelly have. They run in these circles and were able to buy tickets before anyone else.

"Not at all." He nods in the direction the woman went. "I asked the bartender how to get one, and why I wanted it. That woman and her date heard me and she gave it to me."

Wow. Kind people do exist. It's hard to remember that in all the crap that goes on in the world, and the things some of my students have to deal with on a daily basis. But this is completely unexpected. I throw my hands around him, forgetting I have a drink in my hand, spilling a bit of it on the floor. "Thank you so much!"

"I told you I'd do whatever I could." He really didn't do much, but it means the world to me that he was willing to try. "Stay here and I'll grab some napkins to clean that up."

He backs up and finishes his drink, setting it on a table as he makes his way to the bar.

I don't know what I did to deserve him coming back into my life, but I'm grateful. These are the small things nobody I dated before would do. The comparisons I made between them and Patrick. Even when we were friends as kids, he always made sure I didn't want for anything. Constantly going out of his way, and doing odd jobs, to give me the world. And here he is, fifteen years since speaking to each other, doing it again.

Someone taps on my shoulder and I turn toward them. "It's your turn."

"Oh, thank you." I was so busy watching Patrick I hadn't realized the line moved forward. Taking a few steps forward, I approach the table. None of this is real, I know that. At least, I'm pretty sure it's not. I don't want to say one way or another. Everyone has their own beliefs. But it's fun, and maybe I'll get some insight about what I should do with this new development between me and Patrick.

"Please, sit down." The woman gestures to the chair in front of her. "I'm sensing a conflict in your life."

Woah, talk about hitting the nail on the head. I'm sure everyone has some sort of conflict going on, but it feels pretty acute for me since Patrick leaves in a few short days. "How did you know?"

"It's my job," she shrugs her shoulders, "would you like a card reading?"

"Um, sure." I don't know what to expect. I've only seen this done in movies. Or, on the drunken occasion when Hannah and Kelly have dragged me to the French Quarter for a weekend of partying.

"Okay. Touch the top of the deck to put your energy

into the card, and think of a question in your mind while I shuffle the cards."

I do as she asks and lightly touch the card deck. I know I don't have to close my eyes, but I do anyway because I feel absolutely ridiculous watching her shuffle the cards.

When I open them, she has the cards in her hand. "Would you like to pull them or do you want me to?"

"You please. I have no idea what I'm doing."

The first card she pulls is Death. What in the world does that mean? All I know is that it doesn't necessarily mean actual death. Could it be my budding relationship with Patrick? I have no idea.

The next card is ten of swords. The last card she flips over is The Lovers. She sucks in a breath. I'm not sure if she does this for dramatic effect, or if this means something, but it's worrisome either way.

"Is that bad?"

She looks over the cards before answering my question. "The death card could mean that you shut the door on something in your past. It doesn't always mean literal death."

She's not wrong there. When Patrick told me he loved me as teens, I freaked out and practically slammed the door in his face. "What else?"

"The ten of swords could mean exhaustion or the end of something in your present."

The end of something? Does that mean whatever is going on between me and Patrick is doomed before it begins? "Okay."

"The Lovers represent a choice when it comes to a relationship. The choice will be up to you."

Because that isn't cryptic. How is the choice up to me? Last time I checked two people make the choice. But I guess we'll have to wait and see how this plays out between me and Patrick.

"Thank you." I pull my small wallet out of my pocket, grab a few dollars, and tuck it into her tip jar.

"No problem. You just have to decide what is going to lead you to true happiness."

Again cryptic. Nodding, I get off my chair and notice Patrick cleaning up the spill I made. He truly is one of the kindest men I know. He cleaned it up to make sure nobody slips in it. I could have done it, but he knew how much I wanted to do this. This can't be the end of us seeing each other.

Within a few steps, I'm by his side. "How did it go?"

Unsure of how to answer that, I shrug. "It went okay. It was fun." It's the most generic answer I can think of to give him without freaking him out. But it seems to satisfy him.

He grabs my hand and leads me down the stairs of the platform. The DJ shifts gears and plays a slow song. "Would you like to dance?"

"I thought you didn't dance. That's what you told me all throughout high school. At prom and any parties we went to."

He winks at me and pulls me toward the dance floor. "Tonight, I'm making an exception."

My hand moves to his shoulder and his grabs my waist, pulling me close. Screw what the cards said. There's no way I'm letting this end. Because this, right now, feels perfect and exactly how we're meant to be.

15

patrick

JAYLEN in my arms like this is the only thing I've dreamed of since I was a teenager. Tonight, has shown what could have been between us for the past fifteen years. We sway back and forth to the music. Everyone else fades away and it's me and her.

"This has been fun. Thank you for thinking of me."

"Thank you for taking the ticket last minute." She's still going with that story. I'll let her have it even though I know she's full of shit.

The song comes to a close, and I twirl her before dipping her. She wobbles a fraction because of the heels, but I won't let her fall. "Want to get out of here?"

"I thought you'd never ask." She laughs as I pull her back to standing. "I can't wait to get out of these shoes."

Moving us off the dance floor, I find a space without anyone around. "Take them off."

"What? I can't walk through here barefoot."

"You won't be." She gives me a look like I've lost my mind, but slips off her heels. "Hop on my back."

Bending down, I wait for her to grab onto my neck. "We'll look ridiculous."

"Who cares? We're leaving." Finally, she puts her arms around my neck and her legs wrap around my waist as I stand. "There's no point in your feet hurting even more when I'm perfectly capable of carrying you."

"I guess you're making good on your promise."

"You're damn right." I chuckle. At least she remembered that.

I weave my way around people, trying to give enough space so her wings don't knock anyone out. Hannah and Kelly are with the guys they were dancing with in the corner of the room. They wave at us, and I nod my head toward them. Jaylen lifts one hand, and I assume she waves goodbye.

A few more minutes and we're outside. Valet is only a few more steps, and I grab hold of Jaylen's legs with one hand so I can dig in my pocket for the ticket. While waiting, I take her to a ledge nearby and set her down.

"We should probably get these wings off you before they get back with the truck."

"Good idea." I stand behind her and slide the wings off her shoulders. This would be so much better if we could do this in the room. But her wings won't fit in the cab while I'm trying to drive. As soon as they are off, she fumbles in her skirt to turn the lights off. It does nothing to dull her shine.

The valet pulls around with the truck, and I lift her off her feet, cradling her close to me. The attendant opens the passenger side door, and I slide her in before setting the wings in the backseat. By the time I get to the driver's side, she has the GPS pulled up for the hotel.

"Looks like we should be there in about five minutes."

"Good." I tip the valet and put the truck in drive. I can't wait for us to get to the hotel.

* * *

"Did Kelly tell you the room number?" I have both of our bags slung over our shoulder. Jaylen found a pair of flip flops in her bag and slid those on before we got here.

"No, but it should be written on the card." She pulls it out of her pocket and studies it. "It looks like we're on the fifth floor."

I press the up button and we wait for the elevator. It feels like it's taking forever to get here. Finally, the doors open and I usher Jaylen inside before pressing the number five on the panel.

"Your feet doing, okay?"

"Yep." She moves closer to me and wraps an arm around my waist. "Thank you for carrying me out."

"I'll carry you anywhere." It's not a lie. We still have to figure out how we're going to make this work beyond my time here, but I have no doubt we can.

The elevator opens on our floor, and with another look at the keycard, Jaylen leads us in the direction of our room. The halls are quiet, but music can be heard all around us. It's a festive night in the city.

She swipes the card on the door and pushes it open. There's a bottle of wine, two glasses, and various snacks sitting on top of the dresser. Looks like her friends planned our entire evening for us.

"Well, the girls were presumptions." She shakes her

head and pushes the door closed once I'm inside. A part of me assumed they would get us two beds, but nope a king bed fills the center of the room.

"Might as well put it to use." I set our bags down beside the bed and lead Jaylen to it. "You sit. I'll pour us a glass of wine."

"You're just out here breaking all your rules."

"What do you mean?"

"You went to a huge event. You danced in front of people. And you've drunk everything except for beer while we've been out." She ticks off each thing on her fingers. "It's like I don't know who you are anymore."

Luckily, Hannah and Kelly had the forethought to leave a corkscrew. I open the bottle of wine, let it breathe for a minute, and pour it into the glasses. Turning to her, I hold one glass out. "I don't think you realize the things I would do for you."

"Believe me, I know," she sighs. "I was just too young to realize it when we were graduating."

Shrugging my shoulder, I sit down beside her and take a sip from the glass. It's like drinking juice, and I know it's exactly what she likes. "We're older now. We have a perspective we didn't have before."

"Yes, we do." She slides my glass of wine out of my hand and sets them on the dresser. When she turns around, she's pulling the halo headband out of her long brown hair. The gems reflecting the dim hotel light. "We don't have to figure the rest out, but tonight we can start fresh."

She pulls me up and starts unbuttoning my shirt. Placing my hands over hers, I stop her. "We don't have to do this tonight. I was joking earlier."

"I wasn't." She shakes my hands off of hers and continues unbuttoning the shirt and slides it down. She makes a nose of frustration when she realizes I have a white shirt underneath. While I can say this side of her is a surprise to some extent, I know better than to argue. When she wants something, she goes after it with everything she has. I'm considering myself lucky it's me she wants.

16

jaylen

THIS IS TOO FORWARD. It's something I would have done in my youth, but not in the past couple of years. I almost let him stop me, but I can't. He needs to know that I want to be with him. This is something that should have happened long ago. In all honesty, he probably should have been my first instead of the asshole I let take my virginity sophomore year.

I slide my hands down his chest until I reach the bottom of his undershirt and yank it over his head. He helps by lifting his arms. His breathing is heavy, and I know he wants this as badly as I do. He's just too much of a gentleman to say it aloud.

My fingers fumble with the button on his jeans, but when I finally get them loose, I slide them down until he kicks off his boots and steps out of them. He's in nothing but his boxers, and soon he won't be in those. Before I can pull them down, he places his hands over my hands. "My turn."

He hooks his fingers into the sides of my skirt and slowly drags it down my legs. The scratchy tulle adding to the friction of his fingers. I should have thought through the bodysuit when I decided on this costume. But he takes it in stride. He softly grabs the edge of the sleeves, and pulls down until my arms are free and I help him push it the rest of the way down. Kicking the bodysuit to the side, we stand there, staring at each other. Eyes wide, focusing on the reality of what's about to happen. No matter what, tonight changes everything.

He pulls me to him and places soft kisses along my jawline. The scruff on his chin is rough and exhilarating at the same time. Turning me around until my back is to the bed, he lowers me gently onto the mattress. His lips move to my neck and his fingers slide their way down my chest, over my stomach, and lower until his hand covers my already soaked panties. "Oh my God," he whispers against my skin.

Pushing my panties to the side, he slips one finger inside me. Nobody I have ever dated thought of doing foreplay. It went from kissing straight to sex. That could be why I've never felt satisfied with anyone.

I slide my hand into his boxers, my thumb rubbing the tip of his cock before sliding down. He rocks into my hand, and I didn't think anything could excite me the way his soft moans are right this very minute. He lifts up until his mouth meets mine. His tongue dancing with my own. The kiss deepens with the rhythm of our hands until I can't take it anymore.

"I need you." My voice a loud whisper in the quiet room.

"Give me two seconds." He pulls away, and I miss the contact already. He grabs for his pants, pulls out his wallet, and finds a condom tucked away. I don't even want to think he's had that there before tonight. He pushes his boxers down and slides the condom onto his cock. I've never actually watched anyone do that. Most of my encounters have been in a dark room because I didn't want the guy of the time to see all of me.

But with Patrick, all the self-consciousness falls away. If anyone can see past all my imperfections, it's him. He comes back to the bed, pulling my panties down and throwing them somewhere in the room.

"Are you sure?" His voice is gruff. He's giving me another chance to stop this. To change the trajectory of the night, but it's too late. I'm all in.

Nodding, I spread my legs wider, making room for him. He leans over me. One hand beside my head and the other lining himself up to me. He's probably thought about this night more than I ever have. But I know I can't go another day without feeling what it's like to be with this man.

I brush my hands along his sides and he flinches. I forgot how ticklish he is. Holding back a smile, I move my hands to his ass and pull him toward me. He rocks into me until we get into rhythm with each other.

This is how it's always supposed to have been. Me and him. It took me fifteen years to realize that, and now I don't know how I'll be able to let him leave. To go back to my day-to-day life while he's in Texas, so very far away from me.

It's not long before both of us are panting. Whispering each other's names into the night. He rocks faster until my world explodes and all I can see is him. He follows along soon after.

He moves to take care of the condom and I run to the restroom. Tonight, has been everything I hoped it would be. I can only hope we can figure the rest out.

* * *

A loud whisper wakes me up. Patrick is on the phone pacing in front of the bed. When he realizes I'm awake, he tells whoever is on the phone to hold on. He covers the speakers, and comes to sit by me. "I didn't mean to wake you up."

"It's fine," I point toward his phone, "I'll get ready while you finish up your call."

He gives me a quick peck on top of my head and waits until I'm in the restroom to speak again. He doesn't sound happy, and I can't help but feel like our time has come to an end.

I pull the gems out of my hair and turn on the shower. Luckily, the hotel comes with toiletries because I don't want to go back out there and get my own. Making quick work of bathing and washing my hair, I step out of the shower and wrap myself in a towel.

When I open the door, he's no longer on the phone, but he's changed and throws his clothes into a bag. "Is everything okay?"

He glances up at me and does his best to hide his frustration. "I hate to do this, but I need to take you home and haul ass to Texas. One of our food vendors is being an asshole and refuses to deal with anyone but me."

"Is there anything I can do?"

"Not really."

"Okay." I get dressed in the leggings and oversized shirt Kelly packed for me. After running a brush through my hair, I put my stuff in my bag and text Kelly letting her know we're checking out. She doesn't respond. I didn't expect her to. She's most likely sleeping off a hangover.

"You ready?"

Nodding I grab my bag and throw it over my shoulder.

It's not long before he's dropping me off at my house. He walks me to my door and leans in to give me a kiss. I back away and see the pain flicker across his face. "I'm so sorry. I'll make it up to you, I promise."

"It's fine. I guess I'll see you at the next reunion." It's a shitty remark, but I have to protect my heart. He doesn't come home, and I can't leave right now.

"Jay, don't do this. We can make long distance work until we figure things out."

"Okay." It's all I can say right now. Who's to say he won't forget all about me for another fifteen years. It's partially my fault, I know that. But knowing he's leaving again feels like a knife to the heart. "Call me when you get home."

"I will." He leans down and presses a kiss to the top of my head. Somehow knowing what I need at this very moment. My heart squeezes as I watch him get into his truck and back out of my driveway.

17

patrick

I DON'T EVEN BOTHER GOING to my house. I've had hours to play over the last interaction I had with Jaylen this morning. Her being upset is perfectly fine, but when she pulled away from me. That was a kick to the gut. And her dig about me not coming back until the next reunion was completely valid. What else could she think? I stayed away for fifteen years.

Parking in my normal spot, I turn off the truck and slam my door shut. My feet hit hard against the pavement as I storm into Out of the Ashes. Eric sees me and motions me toward the office. He knows the conversation we're about to have, is best behind closed doors.

I close the door behind me and whirl on him. "What the fuck happened?" It's not often I lose my temper, but this has put a kink in the relationship I was trying to build while I was back home.

Eric raises his hands in defense. As if I would actually hit him. I'm not that big of a dick. "Viv placed the food order, but when it got here it wasn't right. The vendor said she got it wrong, and she said he did. I tried to smooth things out, but he won't talk to anyone but you and Angie."

"Well, where's Angie?" This is her bar. She should be here to handle it.

"Dylan's mom had a nasty fall, and they had to take her to hospital in Dallas." Fuck. Now I feel like an even bigger asshole.

"What about Carlos?"

"The vendor doesn't like dealing with him either. He said that Carlos has an attitude problem." Before he met Caroline, maybe. Now, he's probably the calmest person here aside from Eric. "Fine. I'll call him."

"I'm sorry, man." Eric takes a couple of steps toward me before he stops. "I did everything I could to keep from calling you. I know you were trying to work things out with the girl who got away. How did that go?"

I take a few deep breaths. It's not his fault. He tried all the right avenues, and I know that. As annoying as he is, he's a good manager. "It was going great until you called me this morning. Now I'm pretty sure she thinks I'm never coming back."

"Are you?" He looks around. "Aside from this inconvenience, we managed fine without you."

"To see her, yes." I plan on leaving as soon as I get this sorted out. There are still a few more days until I am supposed to be back. "But I don't know that I'd ever move back there. I could get a job in New Orleans, but that isn't my scene."

"You'd be surprised what you would do for love." He's speaking from experience. He got two teenagers when he and Joan made things official.

"True." I run my hand through my hair. "Is it busy out there? I didn't even bother looking."

"Nope. It's a slow day, thank God."

"Good." I grab the phone off the office desk. "Can you search around for other food vendors? I'm going to check the list Vivian sent over and we're likely going to find a new vendor. I just have to run it by Angie and Carlos."

"Absolutely." He gives me a salute before he walks out the office door, closing it behind him.

This is such a mess. But as soon as I meet with this guy, I'm getting in my truck and driving straight to Jaylen's.

* * *

Meeting with the food vendor did not go over well. I confirmed Vivian's order. It was correct, what he sent over wasn't right at all. Needless to say, we don't have a choice but to go with someone else. I refuse to let my cooks be treated the way he treated me and her. Maybe Hudson is right. I do have the patience of a saint. Because I wanted to punch that guy.

Rubbing my temples, I shoot a text to Angie and Carlos letting them know what's going on. I have a list of possible vendors printed out, and meetings set up with them for Monday morning.

It's already almost five and I'm not going to get to Louisiana until late. As much as I hate fast food I'll grab something on the road. I push the chair back and close down the computer. These are Monday problems and I have no intention of dealing with any of them right now.

I walk out of the office, down the hall, and into the bar. What the hell? I blink my eyes to make sure what I'm seeing is real. "Jaylen, what are you doing here?"

"I felt bad for what I said this morning."

"So, you drove all the way here? You could have called."

Eric's eyes are bouncing between me and her. We also have the attention of the entire bar. "You didn't text me letting me know you got here. I assumed you were pissed, and had every right to be. I wanted...I needed to make sure you were okay."

I close the distance between us. "I'm fine. I was actually about to get on the road and head in your direction. You're it for me. Always have been. I know our locations aren't ideal, but we'd make it work."

"I know that." She places her hands on my chest. "I knew that as soon as you dropped me off, but my heart was a different matter entirely. Is there somewhere we can talk privately?" She glances around the bar, all eyes on us.

Nodding, I grab her hand and pull her into the kitchen. "I'm sorry you came all this way."

"Don't be," she leans against the sink, "I actually have a secret. I've been applying to schools in this area for months all in the hopes we could make things work."

"Oh yeah?" I move directly in front of her. Arms on either side.

"Yep. And if you'll have me for the weekend. I want to explore your town."

"I plan on having you for more than the weekend." I lean down and press my lips against hers. Grateful we're going to work this out.

She pulls away and her eyes lock on mine. "Good because I plan on having you forever."

After all this time, I thought she didn't care about me. Maybe I should have gone home sooner because now we have a lot of lost time to make up for.

epilogue

THERE'S a knock at the door. "Jaylen are you expecting someone?"

She comes out of the room in a the same costume she wore the night we reconnected. "No. We have the thing at the bar tonight. Why would I invite anyone?"

"Maybe it's a group of kids looking for candy."

It's still early in the day. The only reason I'm even home is because we shut down the bar early for the event happening tonight. I hate these parties Stella insists on having for the community during every holiday, but Jaylen will be there this year handing out candy, so it won't be so bad.

"Well," she moves toward the front door. "We better not keep them waiting."

She opens the door and squealing commences. What the hell? I move from the living room to the door. Standing in the doorway are Kelly and Hannah. They are jumping up and down with Jaylen between them.

"What are y'all doing here?" My tone may be a little terse, but them being here is completely unexpected.

The noise stops, and three sets of eyes are focused on me. "We wanted to celebrate Halloween with y'all. It's the weekend and we don' have to be at work until Monday morning."

"Oh." It's difficult to keep up the charade of not knowing they were coming. I've never been great about hiding what I'm thinking or feeling. Which is probably why everyone at work thought I was unapproachable. "We have to go to work a thing at the bar I work at tonight, but y'all are more than welcome to come."

"They're definitely coming." Jaylen beams. "I'm so happy you're here. Do you have costumes?"

"Yep," Hannah nods. "They are in the car with our bags."

"I'll grab those for y'all." I take the keys Kelly holds out and move toward the door. "I'll have to leave in a bit, but y'all can ride with Jaylen. She's volunteering so she doesn't have to be there as early as I do."

"Sounds good." She gives me a wink before turning back to her best friend.

Her car is parked on the curb, and I rush over to pull her bags out of the truck. My phone dings in my pocket, and I check to see who it is.

Hudson: We're about thirty minutes away.

Patrick: What about mine and Jaylen's parents?

Hudson: Right behind us.

Patrick: Okay, cool. The girls just showed up.

Hudson: Do we have time to freshen up?

Patrick: Yeah. I'm still trying to figure out how I'm going to sneak y'all into the bar.

Hudson: Let us know when you do.

I slide my phone back in my pocket and get the bags out of the trunk. What in the hell did they pack in these things?

They're only here for a few days. If my bag weighed this much, it'd be for a month long excursion.

As soon as I'm inside, I hurry to the bedroom door and knock. I don't know what they're doing, and I'm not one to barge in. Jaylen opens the door and lets me in.

"Here are your bags." I set them on the bed. "I have to get going. I'll see y'all at the party."

Jaylen wraps her arms around me and gives me a quick kiss. "We'll be there shortly. Love you."

"Love you, too." I'm still in awe that we've reconnected after all these years and are actually together. Never in my wildest dreams did I think that would happen.

* * *

The Halloween party is going well. As much as I gripe about them, Stella knows what she's doing to draw in a crowd. We have stuff on the sidewalk for families and inside for those that want to hang out with other adults.

My phone rings and I rush to answer it. "Hello?"

"Hey," Hudson says. "We're almost to the bar. Do you have a route for us to take?"

"Park on the side of the building and go through the alley to back door. Someone will meet you over there."

"What do I do about the ring?"

"Bring it with you." I swear he doesn't think things through before he speaks. "I'll grab it from you when you get inside."

"Cool. See you in a bit."

"Hey, Viv," I call out to the other chef. "I need to talk to Stella. Do you have everything under control in here?"

"Yep. Do your thing."

I don't know why I bother asking. She's been a great

addition to the crew and handles everything with perfection.

I weave through patrons trying to find the woman putting on this shindig, but run into Angie instead.

"Hey, Boss, my friends and family are here for the thing. I told them to come in through the alley. Can you let them in?"

"I really hate it when you call me that. It makes me feel old."

"You are older than me."

"Barely," she scoffs. "I'll let them in. Just give me the signal when you're ready."

"I will."

Heading back to the kitchen I help Vivian with an order, but it's no use because I'm staring out the door to see when my friends make it in. This is the longest five minutes of my entire life.

"Would you get in here?" Vivian whisper yells. "Everything will be fine."

"Easy for you to say."

She shrugs her shoulder and hands me an order. "Do something to keep your mind busy."

I'm working on an appetizer when Angie comes to the back with Hudson in tow. "The package has been safely delivered."

"Thanks. Can you make sure everyone else is peppered throughout the dance area? I don't want Jaylen to see them until it's time."

"You got it."

Hudson waits for her to leave before he pulls a box out of his pocket. "Here you go. Do I need to do anything else?"

"Can you text Kelly and let her know everything is in

place?"

"Yep." He pulls out his phone and taps on the screen. "Done. I'll go find a place for myself."

Vivian finishes up the orders we've received and calls for the rest of the kitchen staff to take a break in the main area. All of them are grinning as they make their way out of the kitchen.

"I don't know if I can do this."

"Yes, you can." She places her hands on my shoulders. "Take a deep breath." She doesn't move until I do as she says. "Now, get out there and pop the question."

She leaves and I'm the only one in the kitchen now. I take a couple more deep breaths to calm my nerves before straightening my shoulders and walking out of my domain. Time to get the show on the road.

I push my way through the crowd yet again. This time I check my surroundings to make sure Kelly and Hannah have my girlfriend in place.

Doubt creeps in because I've never done anything publicly like this. Even though I was one of the starting players back in high school, I never had to talk to anyone. I didn't make grand gestures. But I feel like Jaylen deserves this. I stepped out of my comfort zone last year when she invited me to a party. I'll do the same now when I ask her to be my wife.

Jaylen is in the middle of the dance floor with her friends twirling around her to the music. I slow my steps so I can approach as the song ends. The DJ has already been asked not to play another song once he seems me.

I lift my arm in the air to signal him as I get closer. He nods that he has the message. The music begins fading out, and the crowd looks to the DJ to see what's happening.

"We are going to take a quick pause on the spooky

festivities for a small announcement. Everyone give it up for Patrick."

All I feel is hundreds of eyes focused on me. I'm doing my best to keep from turning around and bolting for the kitchen. Deep breaths. That's what will get me through this.

Jaylen is searching through the crowd and once her eyes meet mine, everyone else melts away. It's only me and her on this dance floor. Our friends and family make their way to the front, and that's my cue.

As I bend down on one knee, I open the box and present it to her.

"Jaylen, I never thought you'd be a part of my life again. You were and have been the only woman for me. Last year at the reunion, you made me take a chance, and I'm hoping you'll take a chance on me this year."

Her hands cover her mouth and her eyes shine with unshed tears. God, I hope that's a good sign.

"Will you do me the honor of being my wife?"

Instead of answering, she launches herself at me. I topple backward, and I'm pretty sure something on her costume shatters.

"Yes. A million times, yes." Her lips meet mine to applause and whistles coming from everyone in the room.

Someone shakes Jaylen's shoulder and she pulls away from me.

Kelly laughs. "I think maybe you should stand up now. We don't want things to go any further in public or you'll be part of the town gossip."

"Yeah, sorry about that." She grabs Kelly's hand to help her stand.

I stand at the same time as she gasps.

"What's wrong?" I wrap an arm around her waist.

"How are my parents here? And your parents?"

"I may have let them in on the proposal." I pull her tighter to me.

She turns to face me. "You set up all of this?"

"Well, not the Halloween party, no. That's kind of a thing here. But everything else."

Her lips crash into mine once again, but she pulls away before it becomes awkward for everyone to watch.

"I never would have thought you'd make a proposal such a big thing. Or surprise me as much as you did."

I pull her closer as our family descends on us. "Well, expect many more surprises."

Do I know how I'll top this in the future? Absolutely not. But I'm ready to spend my life trying.

also by katrina marie

Do you want to meet more of the characters in Asheville? You can check out my books here. Or, scan the QR code to find out what some of the other residents of this small town are up to.

about the author

Katrina Marie lives in the Dallas area with her husband, two children, grand baby, and fur baby. She is a lover of all things geeky and nerdy. When she's not writing you can find her at her daughter's sporting events, playing with the grand, or curled up reading a book.

You can find Katrina Marie online in the following places:
Sign up for my newsletter: https://www.subscribepage.com/KatrinaMarieNewsletter
Website: katrinamarieauthor.com

facebook.com/katrinamarieauthor

instagram.com/katrinamarieauthor

bookbub.com/profile/katrina-marie

pinterest.com/katrinamarieauthor

tiktok.com/@katrinamarieauthor

patreon.com/katrinamarie